CooL MikE

Written and Illustrated by

Hadori the Author

XULON PRESS

This short children's book is about an eight-year-old boy named Michael Story, otherwise known as "Cool Mike." He is "cool" because he excels in his classes, helps his friends and family with tasks, and is nice to others.

Mike teaches students in his elementary school, as well as all ages, that in order to be cool, you must first be thoughtful, kind, productive, and studious.

Xulon Press
2301 Lucien Way #415
Maitland, FL 32751
407.339.4217
www.xulonpress.com

© 2020 by Hadori the Author

Paperback ISBN-13: 978-1-6628-0620-9

Hardcover ISBN-13: 978-1-6628-0663-6

Ebook ISBN-13: 978-1-6628-0621-6

This book is dedicated to my nieces and nephews.

There once was a boy named Mike who was really cool.

He had the best of times with his family and school.

When the pages start turning, you'll see what I mean.

By the end of the story, you'll want to be on his team.

Mike had a math test and needed to study.
He turned off the TV and began to get ready.
He took out his math book and started addition,

Subtraction, multiplication, then on to division.
Numbers on numbers and problems on problems;
When the test finally came, Mike knew how to solve them.

Mike got an A+ and this was amazing.

When he showed his friends, they stood there gazing.

"An A+?! That's so cool!" said his friend Stew.

Even the skater kid said, "That's radical, dude!!"

Page Three

Mike left with a smile, on his face and in his heart.

He felt good with his grade; it was a very good start.

When Mike got home, he still had his smile.
His mother saw him and stared for a while.
Mike told her his grade and she gave him a hug,
"I'm proud of you, son," she said with much love.

"But I need your help to clean the house:
The laundry, the dishes, and I think I saw a mouse."
Mike went to the closet and picked up the broom.
"I'll help you, Mom; I'll start with my room!"

The next day at school, Mike sat there in class.
He looked at the clock; time was moving so fast.
The teacher gave math problems for the last thing to do.
All of the kids sighed "Aaaawww," because they did not want to.
A student named Sandy sat there and worried.
She needed a pencil and she needed to hurry.

Mike saw what she needed, whispered, and said,
"Here you are, Sandy; I'll use a black pen instead."
Sandy said, "Thank you Mike," and started her work.
"You're welcome!" he said, with a friendly, old smirk.

When class was over, Mike walked out the door.
To his surprise, right there in the hall, he saw a little boy on the floor.
He was pushed to the ground by a bully named Tom.
And while down on the ground, he was yelling for his mom.
Mike walked up to the bully, tapped him on the shoulder, and said,
"Don't push him down, lift him instead."

The bully walked away with a scowl on his face.
So Mike helped the boy up,
Because he felt it was his place.

Now that we see what Mike has done,

We will see what he gets back, one by one.

Kindness is dear; treat it as treasure.

Mike started off good, but he'll end even better.

Mike's teacher noticed how well he had studied.
With grades like this, he wasn't just lucky.
He put in hard work, so there was no stress.
And as a reward, she gave him extra recess.

An hour more to play on the slide:
The jungle gym, monkey bars, and a blue bike to ride.
Mike felt he was dreaming or had made a wish.
How could life get much better than this?

Mike and his mother finished cleaning the house.
They cleaned every corner and there wasn't a mouse.
"Since you got an A+ and made our home clean,
Would you like to go out and get some ice cream?"

Mom said this and gave him a tight hug.
"You're the best mom!" Mike said, as she squeezed him so snug.

Lunch time came one Tuesday afternoon.
It was right after free time and watching cartoons.
Mike looked in his bookbag and to his surprise,
He forgot his lunchbox and started to cry.

He had no food and was very hungry.
A student saw him crying; it was his friend Sandy.
Mike told her what happened. She said, "No need to fear;
I have food for us both and we'll eat it right here."

When Mike was about to get on the bus,

He was pulled from behind by a bully named Guss.

Guss was Tom's brother and was really mad,

Because Mike stopped Tom from hurting the young lad.

Mike got pushed and started to fall,

But was suddenly caught by a student named Paul.

He heard about Mike and the good deeds he's done.

"He shouldn't be bullied because Mike's number one!"

Paul stood up for Mike and so did Mike's friends.

The bullies ran away and this is how the story ends.

Be cool like Mike and you will be fine.
Make good grades, share, and, to all, be kind.
Never forget, as long as you live,
It's great to get, but it's better to give.

15

CPSIA information can be obtained
at www.ICGtesting.com
Printed in the USA
LVHW011615280121
677618LV00009B/389